CITADEL OF
LOST SHIPS

Hardcover ISBN 13: 978-1-5154-4967-6
Trade Paperback ISBN 13: 978-1-5154-4968-3
E-book ISBN 13: 978-1-5154-4969-0

CITADEL OF LOST SHIPS

by Leigh Brackett

It was a Gypsy world, built of space flotsam, peopled with the few free races of the Solar System. Roy Campbell, outcast prey of the Coalition, entered its depths to seek haven for the Kraylens of Venus—only to find that it had become a slave trap from which there was no escape.

Roy Campbell woke painfully. His body made a blind, instinctive lunge for the control panel, and it was only when his hands struck the smooth, hard mud of the wall that he realized he wasn't in his ship any longer, and that the Spaceguard wasn't chasing him, their guns hammering death.

He leaned against the wall, the perspiration thick on his heavy chest, his eyes wide and remembering. He could feel again, as though the running fight were still happening, the bucking of his sleek Fitz-Sothern beneath the calm control of his hands. He could remember the pencil rays lashing through the night, searching for him, seeking his life. He could recall the tiny prayer that lingered in his memory, as he fought so skillfully, so dangerously, to evade the relentless pursuer.

Then there was a hazy period, when a blasting cannon had twisted his ship like a wind-tossed leaf, and his head had smashed cruelly against the control panel. And then the slinking minutes when he had raced for safety—and then the sodden hours when sleep was the only thing in the Universe that he craved.

He sank back on the hide-frame cot with something between a laugh and a curse. He was sweating, and his wiry body twitched. He found a cigarette, lit it on the second try and sat still, listening to his heartbeats slow down.

He began to wonder, then, what had wakened him.

CITADEL OF LOST SHIPS

It was night, the deep indigo night of Venus. Beyond the open hut door, Campbell could see the *liha*-trees swaying a little in the hot, slow breeze. It seemed as though the whole night swayed, like a dark blue veil.

For a long time he didn't hear anything but the far-off screaming of some swamp-beast on the kill. Then, sharp and cruel against the blue silence, a drum began to beat.

It made Campbell's heart jerk. The sound wasn't loud, but it had a tight, hard quality of savagery, something as primal as the swamp and as alien, no matter how long a man lived with it.

The drumming stopped. The second, perhaps the third, ritual prelude. The first must have wakened him. Campbell stared with narrow dark eyes at the doorway.

He'd been with the Kraylens only two days this time, and he'd slept most of that. Now he realized, that in spite of his exhaustion, he had sensed something wrong in the village.

Something was wrong, very wrong, when the drum beat that way in the sticky night.

He pulled on his short, black spaceman's boots and went out of the hut. No one moved in the village. Thatch rustled softly in the slow wind, and that was the only sign of life.

Campbell turned into a path under the whispering *liha*-trees. He wore nothing but the tight black pants of his space garb, and the hot wind lay on his skin like soft hands. He filled his lungs with it. It smelled of warm still water and green, growing things, and....

Freedom. Above all, *freedom*. This was one place where a man could still stand on his legs and feel human.

The drumming started again, like a man's angry heart beating out of the indigo night. This time it didn't stop. Campbell shivered. The trees parted presently, showing a round dark hummock.

6

It was lit by the hot flare of burning *liha* pods. Sweet oily smoke curled up into the branches. There was a sullen glint of water through the trees, but there were closer glints, brighter, fiercer, more deadly.

The glinting eyes of men, silent men, standing in a circle around the hummock.

There was a little man crouched on the mound in the center. His skin had the blue-whiteness of skim milk. He wore a kilt of iridescent scales. His face was subtly reptilian, broad across the cheek-bones and pointed below.

A crest of brilliant feathers—they weren't really feathers, but that was as close as Campbell could get—started just above his brow ridges and ran clean down his spine to the waist. They were standing erect now, glowing in the firelight.

He nursed a drum between his knees. It stopped being just a drum when he touched it. It was his own heart, singing and throbbing with the hate in it.

Campbell stopped short of the circle. His nerves, still tight from his near-fatal brush with the Spaceguard, stung with little flaring pains. He'd never seen anything like this before.

The little man rocked slightly, looking up into the smoke. His eyes were half closed. The drum was part of him and part of the indigo night. It was part of Campbell, beating in his blood.

It was the heart of the swamp, sobbing with hate and a towering anger that was as naked and simple as Adam on the morning of Creation.

*

Campbell must have made some involuntary motion, because a man standing at the edge of the hummock turned his head and saw him. He was tall and slender, and his crest was pure white, a sign of age.

He turned and came to Campbell, looking at him with opalescent eyes. The firelight laid the Earthman's dark face in sharp relief, the lean hard angles, the high-bridged nose that had been broken and not set straight, the bitter mouth.

Campbell said, in pure liquid Venusian, "What is it, Father?"

The Kraylen's eyes dropped to the Earthman's naked breast. There was black hair on it, and underneath the hair ran twisting, intricate lines of silver and deep blue, tattooed with exquisite skill.

The old man's white crest nodded. Campbell turned and went back down the path. The wind and the *liha*-trees, the hot blue night beat with the anger and the hate of the little man with the drum.

Neither spoke until they were back in the hut. Campbell lit a smoky lamp. The old Kraylen drew a long, slow breath.

"My almost-son," he said, "this is the last time I can give you refuge. When you are able, you must go and return no more."

Campbell stared at him. "But, Father! Why?"

The old man spread long blue-white hands. His voice was heavy.

"Because we, the Kraylens, shall have ceased to be."

Campbell didn't say anything for a minute. He sat down on the hide-frame cot and ran his fingers through his black hair.

"Tell me, Father," he said quietly, grimly.

The Kraylen's white crest rippled in the lamplight. "It is not your fight."

Campbell got up. "Look. You've saved my neck more times than I can count. You've accepted me as one of your own. I've been happier here than any—well, skip that. But don't say it isn't my fight."

The pale, triangular old face smiled. But the white crest shook.

"No. There is really no fight. Only death. We're a dying tribe, a mere scrap of old Venus. What matter if we die now—or later?"

Campbell lit a cigarette with quick, sharp motions. His voice was hard. "Tell me, Father. All, and quick."

Opalescent eyes met his. "It is better not."

"I said, 'tell me'!"

"Very well." The old man sighed. "You would hear, after all. You remember the frontier town of Lhi?"

"Remember it!" Campbell's white teeth flashed. "Every dirty stone in it, from the pumping conduits on up. Best place on three planets to fence the hot stuff."

He broke off, suddenly embarrassed. The Kraylen said gently,

"That is your affair, my son. You've been away a long time. Lhi has changed. The Terra-Venusian Coalition Government has taken it for the administration center of Tehara Province."

Campbell's eyes, at mention of the Coalition Government, acquired a hot, hard brightness. He said, "Go on."

The old man's face was cut from marble, his voice stiff and distant.

"There have been men in the swamps. Now word has been sent us. It seems there is coal here, and oil, and certain minerals that men prize. They will drain the swamps for many miles, and work them."

Campbell let smoke out of his lungs, very slowly. "Yeah? And what becomes of you?"

The Kraylen turned away and stood framed in the indigo square of the doorway. The distant drum sobbed and shouted. It was hot, and yet the sweat turned cold on Campbell's body.

The old man's voice was distant and throbbing and full of anger, like the drum. Campbell had to strain to hear it.

"They will take us and place us in camps in the great cities. Small groups of us, so that we are divided and split. Many people will pay to see us, the strange remnants of old Venus. They will pay for our skills in the curing of *leshen*-skins and the writing of quaint music, and tattooing. We will grow rich."

Campbell dropped the cigarette and ground it on the dirt floor. Knotted veins stood out on his forehead, and his face was cruel. The old man whispered:

"*We will die first.*"

*

It was a long time since anyone had spoken. The drumming had stopped, but the echo of it throbbed in Campbell's pulses. He looked at his spread, sinewy hands on his knees and swallowed because the veins of his neck were swollen and hurting.

Presently he said, "Couldn't you go further back into the swamps?"

The old Kraylen spoke without moving. He still stood in the doorway, watching the trees sway in the slow wind.

"The Nahali live there. Besides, there is no clean water and no earth for crops. We are not lizard eaters."

"I've seen it happen," said Campbell somberly. "On Earth, and Mars, and Mercury, and the moons of Jupiter and Saturn. Little people driven from their homes, robbed of their way of life, exploited and for the gaping idiots in the trade centers. Little people who didn't care about progress, and making money. Little people who only wanted to live, and breathe, and be let alone."

He got up in a swift savage rush and hurled a gourd of water crashing into a corner and sat down again. He was shivering. The old Kraylen turned.

"Little people like you, my son?"

Campbell shrugged. "Maybe. We'd worked our farm for three hundred years. My father didn't want to sell. They condemned it anyhow. It's under water now, and the dam runs a hell of a big bunch of factories."

"I'm sorry."

Campbell looked up, and his face softened. "I've never understood," he said. "You people are the most law-abiding citizens I ever met. You don't like strangers. And yet I blunder in here, hot on the lam and ugly as a swamp-dragon, and you...."

He stopped. It was probably the excitement that was making his throat knot up like that. The smoke from the lamp stung his eyes. He blinked and bent to trim it.

"You were wounded, my son, and in trouble. Your quarrel with the police was none of ours. We would have helped anyone. And then, while you had fever and your guard was down, you showed that more than your body needed help. We gave you what we could."

"Yeah," said Campbell huskily. He didn't say it, but he knew well enough that what the Kraylens had given him had kept him from blowing his top completely.

Now the Kraylens were going the way of the others, straws swept before the great broom of Progress. Nothing could stop it. Earth's empire surged out across the planets, building, bartering, crashing across time and custom and race to make money and the shining steel cage of efficiency.

A cage wherein a sheep could live happily enough, well-fed and opulent. But Campbell wasn't a sheep. He'd tried it, and he couldn't bleat in tune. So he was a wolf, now, alone and worrying the flock.

Soon there wasn't going to be a place in the Solar System where a man could stand on his own feet and breathe.

He felt stifled. He got up and stood in the doorway, watching the trees stir in the hot indigo gloom. The trees would go. Wells and mines, slag and soot and clattering machinery, and men in sweat-stained shirts laboring night and day to get, to grow, to produce.

Campbell's mouth twisted, bitter and sardonic. He said softly: "God help the unconstructive!"

The old Kraylen murmured, "What happened to those others, my son?"

Campbell's lean shoulders twitched. "Some of them died. Some of them submitted. The rest...."

He turned, so suddenly that the old man flinched. Campbell's dark eyes had a hot light in them, and his face was sharply alive.

"The rest," he said evenly, "went to Romany."

*

He talked, then. Urgently, pacing the hut in nervous catlike strides, trying to remember things he had heard and not been very much interested in at the time. When he was through, the Kraylen said:

"It would be better. Infinitely better. But—" He spread his long pale hands, and his white crest drooped. "But there is no time. Government men will come within three days to take us—that was the time set. And since we will not go...."

Campbell thought of the things that had happened to other rebellious tribes. He felt sick. But he made his voice steady.

"We'll hope it's time, Father. Romany is in an orbit around Venus now—I nearly crashed it coming in. I'm going to try, anyhow. If I don't—well, stall as long as you can."

Remembering the drum and the way the men had looked, he didn't think that would be long. He pulled on a loose shirt of green spider-silk, slung the belt of his heavy needle-gun over one shoulder, and picked up his black tunic.

He put his hand on the Kraylen's shoulder and smiled. "We'll take care of it, Father."

The old man's opalescent eyes were shadowed. "I wish I could stop you. It's hopeless for us, and you are—*hot* is that the word?"

Campbell grinned. "Hot," he said, "is the word. Blistering! The Coalition gets awfully mad when someone pulls their own hi-jacking stunt on them. But I'm used to it."

It was beginning to get light outside. The old man said quietly, "The gods go with you, my son."

Campbell went out, thinking he'd need them.

It was full day when he reached his hidden ship—a sleek, souped-up Fitts-Sothern that had the legs of almost anything in space. He paused briefly by the airlock, looking at the sultry green of *liha*-trees under a pearl-grey sky, the white mist lapping around his narrow waist.

He spent a long time over his charts, feeding numbers to the calculators. When he got a set-up that suited him, he took the Fitts-Sothern up on purring 'copters, angling out over the deep swamps. He felt better, with the ship under his hands.

The Planetary Patrol blanket was thin over the deep swamps, but it was vigilant. Campbell's nerves were tight. They got tighter as he came closer to the place where he was going to have to begin his loop over to the night side.

He was just reaching for the rocket switch when the little red light started to flash on the indicator panel.

Somebody had a detector beam on him. And he was morally certain that the somebody was flying a Patrol boat.

II

There was one thing about the Venusian atmosphere. You couldn't see through it, even with infra-beams, at very long range. The

13

intensity needle showed the Patrol ship still far off, probably not suspicious yet, although stray craft were rare over the swamps.

In a minute the copper would be calling for information, with his mass-detectors giving the Fitts-Sothern a massage. Campbell didn't think he'd wait. He slammed in the drive rockets, holding them down till the tubes warmed. Even held down, they had plenty.

The Fitts-Sothern climbed in a whipping spiral. The red light wavered, died, glowed again. The copper was pretty good with his beam. Campbell fed in more juice.

The red light died again. But the Patrol boat had all its beams out now, spread like a fish net. The Fitts-Sothern struck another, lost it, struck again, and this time she didn't break out.

Campbell felt the sudden racking jar all through him. "Tractor beams," he said. "You think so, buddy?"

The drive jets were really warming now. He shot it to them. The Fitts-Sothern hung for a fractional instant, her triple-braced hull shuddering so that Campbell's teeth rang together.

Then she broke, blasting up right through the netted beams. Campbell jockeyed his port and starboard steering jets. The ship leaped and skittered wildly. The copper didn't have time to focus full power on her anywhere, and low power to the Fitts-Sothern was a nuisance and nothing more.

Campbell went up over the Patrol ship, veered off in the opposite direction from the one he intended to follow, hung in a tight spiral until he was sure he was clean, and then dived again.

The Patrol boat wasn't expecting him to come back. The pilot was concentrating on where Campbell had gone, not where he had been. Campbell grinned, opened full throttle, and went skittering over the curve of the planet to meet the night shadow rushing toward him.

He didn't meet any more ships. He was way off the trade lanes, and moving so fast that only blind luck could tag him. He hoped the Patrol was hunting for him in force, back where they'd lost him. He hoped they'd hunt a long time.

Presently he climbed, on slowed and muffled jets, out of the atmosphere. His black ship melted indistinguishably into the black shadow of the planet. He slowed still more, just balancing the Venus-drag, and crawled out toward a spot marked on his astrogation chart.

An Outer Patrol boat went by, too far off to bother about. Campbell lit a cigarette with nervous hands. It was only a quarter smoked when the object he'd been waiting for loomed up in space.

His infra-beam showed it clearly. A round, plate-shaped mass about a mile in diameter, built of three tiers of spaceships. Hulks, ancient, rusty, pitted things that had died and not been decently buried, welded together in a solid mass by lengths of pipe let into their carcasses.

Before, when he had seen it, Campbell had been in too much of a hurry to do more than curse it for getting in his way. Now he thought it was the most desolate, Godforsaken mass of junk that had ever made him wonder why people bothered to live at all.

He touched the throttle, tempted to go back to the swamps. Then he thought of what was going to happen back there, and took his hand away.

"Hell!" he said. "I might as well look inside."

He didn't know anything about the internal set-up of Romany—what made it tick, and how. He knew Romany didn't love the Coalition, but whether they would run to harboring criminals was another thing.

It wouldn't be strange if they had been given pictures of Roy Campbell and told to watch for him. Thinking of the size of the reward for him, Campbell wished he were not quite so famous.

Romany reminded him of an old-fashioned circular mouse-trap. Once inside, it wouldn't be easy to get out.

"Of all the platinum-plated saps!" he snarled suddenly. "Why am I sticking my neck out for a bunch of semi-human swamp-crawlers, anyhow?"

He didn't answer that. The leading edge of Romany knifed toward him. There were lights in some of the hulks, mostly in the top layer. Campbell reached for the radio.

He had to contact the big shots. No one else could give him what he needed. To do that, he had to walk right up to the front door and announce himself. After that....

The manual listed the wave-length he wanted. He juggled the dials and verniers, wishing his hands wouldn't sweat.

"Spaceship *Black Star* calling Romany. Calling Romany...."

His screen flashed, flickered, and cleared. "Romany acknowledging. Who are you and what do you want?"

*

Campbell's screen showed him a youngish man—a Taxil, he thought, from some Mercurian backwater. He was ebony-black and handsome, and he looked as though the sight of Campbell affected him like stale beer.

Campbell said, "Cordial guy, aren't you? I'm Thomas Black, trader out of Terra, and I want to come aboard."

"That requires permission."

"Yeah? Okay. Connect me with the boss."

The Taxil now looked as though he smelled something that had been dead a long time. "Possibly you mean Eran Mak, the Chief Councillor?"

"Possibly," admitted Campbell, "I do." If the rest of the gypsies were anything like this one, they sure had a hate on for outsiders.

Well, he didn't blame them. The screen blurred. It stayed that way while Campbell smoked three cigarettes and exhausted his excellent vocabulary. Then it cleared abruptly.

Eran Mak sounded Martian, but the man pictured on the screen was no Martian. He was an Earthman, with a face like a wedge of granite and a frame that was all gaunt bones and thrusting angles.

His hair was thin, pale-red and fuzzy. His mouth was thin. Even his eyes were thin, close slits of pale blue with no lashes. Campbell disliked him instantly.

"I'm Tredrick," said the Earthman. His voice was thin, with a sound in it like someone walking on cold gravel. "Terran Overchief. Why do you wish to land, Mister Black?"

"I bring a message from the Kraylen people of Venus. They need help."

Tredrick's eyes became, if possible, thinner and more pale.

"*Help?*"

"Yes. Help." Campbell was struck by a sudden suspicion, something he caught flickering across Tredrick's granite features when he said "Kraylen." He went on, slowly, "The Coalition is moving in on them. I understand you people of Romany help in cases like that."

There was a small, tight silence.

"I'm sorry," said Tredrick. "There is nothing we can do."

17

Campbell's dark face tightened. "Why not? You helped the Shenyat people on Ganymede and the Drylanders on Mars. That's what Romany is, isn't it—a refuge for people like that?"

"As a *latnik*, there's a lot you don't know. At this time, we cannot help anyone. Sorry, Black. Please clear ship."

The screen went dead. Campbell stared at it with sultry eyes. Sorry. The hell you're sorry. What gives here, anyway?

He thrust out an angry hand to the transmitter. And then, quite suddenly, the Taxil was looking at him out of the screen.

The hostile look was gone. Anger replaced it, but not anger at Campbell. The Taxil said, in a low, rapid voice:

"You're not lying about coming from the Kraylens?"

"No. No, I'm not lying." He opened his shirt to show the tattoo.

"The dirty scut! Mister Black, clear ship, and then make contact with one of the outer hulks on the lowest tier. You'll find emergency hatchways in some of the pipes. Come inside, and wait."

His dark eyes had a savage glitter. "There are some of us, Mister Black, who still consider Romany a refuge!"

*

Campbell cleared ship. His nerves were singing in little tight jerks. He'd stepped into something here. Something big and ugly. There had been a certain ring in the Taxil's voice.

The thin, gravelly Mr. Tredrick had something on his mind, too. Something important, about Kraylens. Why Kraylens, of all the unimportant people on Venus?

Trouble on Romany. Romany the gypsy world, the Solar System's stepchild. Strictly a family affair. What business did a Public Enemy with a low number and a high valuation have mixing into that?

Then he thought of the drum beating in the indigo night, and an old man watching *liha*-trees stir in a slow, hot wind.

Roy Campbell called himself a short, bitter name, and sighed, and reached lean brown hands for the controls. Presently, in the infra-field, he made out an ancient Krub freighter on the edge of the lowest level, connected to companion wrecks by sections of twelve-foot pipe. There was a hatch in one of the pipes, with a hand-wheel.

The Fitts-Sothern glided with exquisite daintiness to the pipe, touched it gently, threw out her magnetic grapples and suction flanges, and hung there. The airlock exactly covered the hatchway.

Campbell got up. He was sweating and as edgy as a tomcat on the prowl. With great care he buckled his heavy gun around his narrow hips. Then he went into the airlock.

He checked grapples and flanges with inordinate thoroughness. The hatch-wheel jutted inside. He picked up a spanner and turned it, not touching the frigid metal.

There was a crude barrel-lock beyond. Campbell ran his tongue once over dry lips, shrugged, and climbed in.

He got through into a space that was black as the Coalsack. The air was thin and bitingly cold. Campbell shivered in his silk shirt. He laid his hand on his gun butt and took two cautious steps away from the bulge of the lock, wishing to hell he were some place else.

Cold green light exploded out of nowhere behind him. He half turned, his gun blurring into his palm. But he had no chance to fire it.

Something whipped down across the nerve-center in the side of his neck. His body simply faded out of existence. He fell on his face and lay there, struggling with all his might to move and achieving only a faint twitching of the muscles.

He knew vaguely that someone rolled him over. He blinked up into the green light, and heard a man's deep, soft voice say from the darkness behind it:

"What made you think you could get away with it?"

Campbell tried three times before he could speak. "With what?"

"Spying. Does Tredrick think we're children?"

"I wouldn't know." It was easier to speak this time. His body was beginning to fade in again, like something on a television screen. He tried to close his hand. It didn't work very well, but it didn't matter. His gun was gone.

Something moved across the light. A man's body, a huge, supple, muscular thing the color of dark bronze. It knelt with a terrible tigerish ease beside Campbell, the bosses on its leather kilt making a clinking noise. There was a jeweled gorget of reddish metal around the base of its throat. The stones had a wicked glitter.

The deep, soft voice said, "Who are you?"

Campbell tried to force the returning life faster through his body. The man's face was in shadow. Campbell looked up with sultry, furious eyes and achieved a definite motion toward getting up.

The kneeling giant put out his right arm. The green light burned on it. Campbell's eyes followed it down toward his throat. His face became a harsh, irregular mask cut from dark wood.

The arm was heavily, beautifully muscled. But where the hand should have been there was a leather harness and a hook of polished Martian bronze.

*

Campbell knew what had struck him. The thin, hard curve of that hook, more potent than the edge of any hand.

The point pricked his throat, just over the pulse on the left side. The man said softly:

"Lie still, little man, and answer."

Campbell lay still. There was nothing else to do. He said, "I'm Thomas Black, if that helps. Who are you?"

"What did Tredrick tell you to do?"

"To get the hell out. What gives with you?" If that Taxil was spreading the word about him, he'd better hurry. Campbell decided to take a chance. The guy with the hook didn't seem to love Tredrick.

"The black boy in the radio room told me to come aboard and wait. Seems he's sore at Tredrick, too. So am I. That makes us all pals, doesn't it?"

"You lie, little man." The deep voice was quietly certain. "You were sent to spy. Answer!"

The point of the hook put the exclamation point on that word. Campbell winced away. He wished the lug wouldn't call him "little man." He wouldn't remember ever having felt more hopelessly scared.

He said, "Damn your eyes, I'm not lying. Check with the Taxil. He'll tell you."

"And betray him to Tredrick? You're clumsy, little man."

The hook bit deeper. Campbell's neck began to bleed. He felt all right again otherwise. He wondered whether he'd have a chance of kicking the man in the stomach before his throat was torn out. He tried to draw farther away, but the pipe wall wouldn't give.

A woman's voice spoke then, quite suddenly, from beyond the green light. Campbell jumped. He hadn't even thought about anyone else being there. Now it was obvious that someone was holding the light.

The voice said, "Wait, Marah. Zard is calling me now."

It was a clear, low voice. It had music in it. Campbell would have loved it if it had croaked, but as it was it made his nerves prick with sheer ecstasy.

The hook lifted out of the hole it had made, but it didn't go away. Campbell raised his head a little. The lower edge of the green light spilled across a pair of sandalled feet. The bare white legs above them were as beautiful as the voice, in the same strong clear way.

There was a long silence. Marah, the man with the hook, turned his face partly into the light. It was oblong and scarred and hard as beaten bronze. The eyes in it were smoky ember, set aslant under a tumbled crest of tawny hair.

After a long time the woman spoke again. Her voice was different this time. It was angry, and the anger made it sing and throb like the Kraylen's drum.

"The Earthman is telling the truth, Marah. Zard sent him. He's here about the Kraylens."

The big man—a Martian Drylander, Campbell thought, from somewhere around Kesh—got up, fast. "The Kraylens!"

"He asked for help, and Tredrick sent him away." The light moved closer. "But that's not all, Marah. Tredrick has found out about—us. Old Ekla talked. They're waiting for us at the ship!"

III

Marah turned. His eyes had a greenish, feral glint like those of a lion on the kill. He said, "I'm sorry, little man."

Campbell was on his feet, now, and reasonably steady. "Think nothing of it," he said dourly. "A natural mistake." He looked at the hook and mopped the blood from his neck, and felt sick. He added, "The name's Black. Thomas Black."

"It wouldn't be Campbell?" asked the woman's voice. "Roy Campbell?"

He squinted into the light, not saying anything. The woman said, "You are Roy Campbell. The Spaceguard was here not long ago, hunting for you. They left your picture."

He shrugged. "All right. I'm Roy Campbell."

"That," said Marah softly, "helps a lot!" He could have meant it any way. His hook made a small, savage flash in the green light.

"There's trouble here on Romany. Civil war. Men are going to be killed before it's over—perhaps now. Where's your place in it?"

"How do I know? The Coalition is moving in on the Kraylens. I owe them something. So I came here for help. Help! Yeah."

"You'll get it," said the woman. "You'll get it, somehow, if any of us live."

Campbell raised his dark brows. "What goes on here, anyhow?"

The woman's low voice sang and throbbed against the pipe walls. "A long time ago there were a few ships. Old ships, crowded with people who had no homes. Little, drifting people who made a living selling their odd handicrafts in the spaceports, who were cursed as a menace to navigation and distrusted as thieves. Perhaps they were thieves. They were also cold, and hungry, and resentful.

"After a while the ships began to band together. It was easier that way—they could share food and fuel, and talk, and exchange ideas. Space wasn't so lonely. More and more ships drifted in. Pretty soon there were a lot of them. A new world, almost.

"They called it Romany, after the wandering people of Earth, because they were gypsies, too, in their own way.

"They clung to their own ways of life. They traded with the noisy, trampling people on the planets they had been driven away from because they had to. But they hated them, and were hated, just as gypsies always are.

"It wasn't an easy life, but they were free in it. They could stand anything, as long as they were free. And always, anywhere in the Solar System, wherever some little lost tribe was being swallowed up and needed help, ships from Romany went to help them."

Her voice dropped. Campbell thought again of the Kraylen's drum, singing its anger in the indigo night.

"That was the creed of Romany," she whispered. "Always to help, always to be a refuge for the little people who couldn't adjust themselves to progress, who only wanted to die in dignity and peace. And now...."

"And now," said Marah somberly, "there is civil war."

*

Campbell drew a long, unsteady breath. The woman's voice throbbed in him, and his throat was tight. He said "*Tredrick?*"

Marah nodded. "Tredrick. But it's more than that. If it were only Tredrick, it wouldn't be so bad."

He ran the curve of his hook over his scarred chin, and his eyes burned like candle flames.

"Romany is growing old, and soft. That's the real trouble. Decay. Otherwise, Tredrick would have been kicked into space long ago. There are old men in the Council, Campbell. They think more of comfort than they do of—well...."

"Yeah. I know. What's Tredrick's angle?"

"I don't know. He's a strange man—you can't get a grip on him. Sometimes I think he's working for the Coalition."

Campbell scowled. "Could be. You gypsies have a lot of wild talents and some unique skills—I've met some of 'em. The man that controlled them would be sitting pretty. The Coalition would like it, too."

The woman said bitterly, "And they could always exhibit us. Tours, at so much a head. So quaint—a cross-section of a lost world!"

"Tredrick's the strong man," Marah went on. "Eran Mak is Chief Councillor, but he does as Tredrick tells him. The idea is that if Romany settled down and stops getting into trouble with the

24

Planetary Coalitions, we can have regular orbits, regular trade, and so on."

"In other words," said Campbell dryly, "stop being Romany."

"You understand. A pet freak, a tourist attraction, a fat source of revenue." Again the savage flash of the hook. "A damned circus!"

"And Tredrick, I take it, has decided that you're endangering the future of Romany by rebellion, and put the finger on you."

"Exactly." Marah's yellow eyes were bright and hard, meeting Campbell's.

Campbell thought about the Fitts-Sothern outside, and all the lonely reaches of space where he could go. There were lots of Coalition ships to rob, a few plague-spots left to spend the loot in. All he had to do was walk out.

But there was a woman's voice, with a note in it like a singing, angry drum. There was an old man's voice, murmuring, "Little people like you, my son?"

It was funny, how a guy could be alone and not know he minded it, and then suddenly walk in on perfect strangers and not be alone any more—alone inside, that is—and know that he *had* minded it like hell.

It had been that way with the Kraylens. It was that way now. Campbell shrugged. "I'll stick around."

He added irritably, "Sister, will you for Pete's sake get that light out of my eyes?"

She moved it, shining it down. "The name's Moore. Stella Moore."

He grinned. "Sorry. So you do have a face, after all."

It wasn't beautiful. It was pale and heart-shaped, framed in a mass of unruly red-gold hair. There were long, grey eyes under dark-gold brows that had never been plucked, and a red, sullen mouth.

Her teeth were white and uneven, when she smiled. He liked them. The red of her sullen lips was their own. She wore a short tunic the color of Tokay grapes, and the body under it was long and clean-cut. Her arms and throat had the whiteness of pearl.

Marah said quietly, "Contact Zard. Tell him to throw the PA system wide open and say we're taking the ship, now, to get the Kraylens!"

*

Stella stood absolutely still. Her grey eyes took on an eerie, remote look, and Campbell shivered slightly. He'd seen telepathy often enough in the System's backwaters, but it never seemed normal.

Presently she said, "It's done," and became human again. The green light went out. "Power," she explained. "Besides, we don't need it. Give me your hand, Mister Campbell."

He did, with absolutely no aversion. "My friends," he said, "generally call me Roy." She laughed, and they started off, moving with quick sureness in the black, icy darkness.

The ship, it seemed, was up on the second level, on the edge of the living quarters. Down here was all the machinery that kept Romany alive—heat, light, water, air, and cooling systems—and a lot of storage hulks.

The third tier was a vast hydroponic farm, growing the grain and fruit and vegetables that fed the Romany thousands.

Stumbling through pipes and dismantled hulks that smelled of sacking and dried vegetables and oil, Campbell filled in the gaps.

The leaders of the rebel element had held a meeting down here, in secret. Marah and the girl had been coming from it when Campbell blundered into them. The decision had been to rescue the Kraylens no matter what happened.

They'd known about the Kraylens long before Campbell had. Gypsies trading in Lhi had brought word. Now the Kraylens were a symbol over which two points of view were clashing in deadly earnest.

Remembering Tredrick's thin, harsh face, Campbell wondered uneasily how many of them *would* live to take that ship away.

He became aware gradually of a broken, rhythmic tap and clank transmitted along the metal walls.

"Hammers," said Stella softly. "Hammers and riveters and welders, fighting rust and age to keep Romany alive. There's no scrap of this world that wasn't discarded as junk, and reclaimed by us."

Her voice dropped. "Including the people."

Campbell said, "They're scrapping some beautiful things these days."

She knew what he meant. She even laughed a little. "I was born on Romany. There are a lot of Earth people who have no place at home."

"I know." Campbell remembered his father's farm, with blue cold water over the fields instead of sky. "And Tredrick?"

"He was born here, too. But the taint is in him...." She caught her breath in a sudden sharp cry. "Marah! Marah, *it's Zard!*"

They stopped. A pulse began to beat under Campbell's jaw. Stella whispered, "He's gone. I felt him call, and now he's gone. He was trying to warn us."

Marah said grimly, "Tredrick's got him, then. Probably knocked him out while he was trying to escape from the radio room."

"He was frightened," said Stella quietly. "Tredrick has done something. He wanted to warn us."

Marah grunted. "Have your gun ready, Campbell. We go up, now."

*

27

CITADEL OF LOST SHIPS

They went up a wooden ladder. It was suddenly getting hot. Campbell guessed that Romany was in the sun again. The Martian opened a door at the top, very, very slowly.

A young, vibrant voice sang out, "All clear!" They piled out of the doorway. Four or five husky young Paniki barbarians from Venus stood grinning beside two bound and slumbering Earthmen.

Campbell stared past them. The air was still and hot, hung with veils of steamy mist. There was mossy earth dotted with warm pools. There were *liha*-trees, sultry green under a pearly light that was still brightening out of indigo gloom.

A slow, hot breath of wind stirred the mist and *liha*-trees. It smelt of warm still water and growing things, and—freedom.

Campbell drew a long breath. His eyes stung and the veins in his neck hurt. He knew it was a dead hulk, with an iron sky above the pearl-grey mist. But it smelt of freedom.

He said, "What are we waiting for?"

Marah laughed, and the young Venusian laughed. Barbarians, going to fight and laughing about it. Stella's grey eyes held a sultry flame, and her lips were blood-orange and trembling.

Campbell kissed them. He laughed, too, softly, and said, "Okay, Gypsy. Let's go."

They went, through the seven hulks of the Venusian Quarter. Because of the Kraylens, most of the Venusians were with the rebels, but even so there were angry voices raised, and fists, and a few weapons, and some blood got spilled.

More tow-headed young men joined them, and squat little upland nomads who could talk to animals, and three four-armed, serpentine crawlers from the Lohari swamps.

They came presently to a huge dismantled Hoyt freighter on the edge of the Venusian Quarter. There were piles of goods waiting lading through the row of airlocks into smaller trading ships. Marah stopped, his gorget shooting wicked jeweled sparks in the sunlight that seared in through half-shuttered ports, and the others flowed in behind him.

They were on a narrow gallery about halfway up the inner wall. Campbell looked down. There were people on the ladders and the two balcony levels below. A sullen, ugly mob of people from Earth, from Venus, from Mars and Mercury and the moons of Jupiter and Saturn.

Men and near-men and sheer monstrosities, silent and watching in the hot light. Here a crest of scarlet antennae burning, there the sinuous flash of a scaled back, and beyond that the slow ominous weaving of light-black tentacles.

A creature like a huge blue spider with a child's face let out a shrill unearthly scream. "Traitor! Traitor!"

The whole packed mass on the ladders and the galleries stirred like a weird tapestry caught in a gust of wind. The rushing whisper of their movement, their breathing, and their anger sang across Campbell's nerves in points of fire.

Anger. Anger in the Kraylen's drum and Stella's voice and Marah's yellow eyes. Anger like the sunlight, hot and primal. The anger of little men flogged into greatness.

A voice spoke from across the deck below, cold, clear, without the faintest tremor.

"We want no trouble. Return to your quarters quietly."

"*The Kraylens!*"

The name came thundering out of all those angry throats, beating down against the gaunt, erect figure standing in the forefront of a circle of Earthmen guarding the locks with ready guns.

29

Tredrick's thin, red head never stirred from its poised erectness. "The Kraylens are out of your hands, now. They harbored a dangerous criminal, and they are now being imprisoned in Lhi to answer for it."

Roy Campbell gripped the iron railing in front of him. It seemed to him that he could see, across all that space, the cold, bright flame of satisfaction in Tredrick's eyes.

The thin, calm voice slid across his eardrums with the cruel impersonality of a surgeon's knife.

"That criminal, Roy Campbell, is now on Romany. The Spaceguard is on its way here now. For the sake of the safety of your families, for the future of Romany, I advise no one to hide him or help him escape."

IV

Campbell stood still, not moving or speaking, his hard, dark face lined and dead, like old wood. From a great distance he heard Marah's smothered, furious curse, the quick catch of Stella's breath, the sullen breathing and stirring of the mob that was no longer sure what it wanted to do.

But all he could see was the pale, kind face of an old man smiling in the warm, blue night, and the dirty, sordid stones of Lhi.

A voice spoke, from beside the circle of armed men. Campbell heard it with some part of his brain. An old voice, dry and rustling, possessed of great dignity and great pain.

"My children," it said. "Have patience. Have faith that we, your leaders, have the good of Romany at heart."

Campbell looked with dead, dark eyes at the speaker, standing beside Tredrick. A small man in a robe of white fur. A Martian from one of the Polar Cities, frail, black-eyed grave, and gently strong.

"Remember the cold, the hunger, the uncertainty we have endured. We have a chance now for security and peace. Let there be no trouble, now or when the Spaceguard comes. Return to your quarters quietly."

"Trouble!" Marah's voice roared out across the hot, still air. Every face down there below turned up toward the balcony. Campbell saw Tredrick start, and speak to one of the guards. The guard went out, not too fast. Campbell swore under his breath, and his brain began to tick over again, swift and hard.

Marah thundered on, a bronze Titan in the sultry glare. His gorget, his yellow eyes, the bosses on his kilt held points of angry flame.

"You, Eran Mak, a Martian! Have you forgotten Kesh, and Balakar, and the Wells of Tamboina? Can you crawl to the Coalition like a *sindar* for the sake of the bones they throw you? You, Tredrick! You've sold us out. Since when have *latniks* been called to meddle in Romany's affairs?"

Tredrick's cold voice was quite steady. "The Kraylens are beyond reach, Marah. A revolt will get you nothing. Do you want blood on your hands?"

"My hand," said Marah softly. His hook made a burning, vicious arc in the hot light. "If there's blood on this, the Coalition spilled it when their Frontier Marshal lopped my sword-hand for raising it against him."

The mob stirred and muttered. And Campbell said swiftly, "Tredrick's right. But there's still a chance, if you want to take it."

Stella Moore put a hand on Marah's arm. "How?"

Tredrick was still pretending he hadn't seen Campbell, pretending there weren't men crawling through dark tunnels to trap him.

"It'll mean trouble. It may mean death or imprisonment. It's a million-to-one shot. You'd better give me up and forget it."

CITADEL OF LOST SHIPS

The point of Marah's hook pricked under his jaw. "Speak quickly, little man!"

"Okay. Tell 'em to behave. Then get me out of here, fast!"

*

Tredrick's men knew their way around. A lot of gypsies, moreover, who weren't with Tredrick, joined the hunt for the *latnik*. They didn't want trouble with the Spaceguard.

Campbell stumbled through a maze of dark and stifling passages, holding Stella's hand and thinking of the Spaceguard ships sweeping closer. They were almost caught a dozen times, trying to get across Romany to the Fitts-Sothern.

The hunt seemed to be an outlet for the pent feelings of Romany. Campbell decided he would never go hunting again. And then, just above where his ship lay, they stepped into a trap.

They were in the Saturnian Quarter, in the hulk devoted to refugees from Titan. There were coolers working here. There was snow on the barren rocks, glimmering in weird light like a dark rainbow.

"The caves," said Stella Moore. "The Baraki."

There was an echoing clamor of voices all around them, footsteps clattering over metal and icy rock. They ran, breathing hard. There were some low cliffs, and a ledge, and then caves with queer blue-violet fires burning in them.

Creatures sat at the cave mouths. They were small, vaguely anthropoid, dead white, and unpleasantly rubbery. They were quite naked, and their single eyes were phosphorescent. Marah knelt.

"Little Fathers, we ask shelter in the name of freedom."

The shouts and the footsteps were closer. There was sweat on Campbell's forehead. One of the white things nodded slightly.

"No disturbance," it whispered. "We will have no disturbance of our thoughts. You may shelter, to stop this ugly noise."

"Thank you, Little Father." Marah plunged into the cave, with the others on his heels. Campbell snarled, "They'll come and take us!"

Stella's sullen lips smiled wolfishly. "No. Watch."

The cave, the violet fire were suddenly gone. There was a queer darkness, a small electric shiver across Campbell's skin. He started, and the girl whispered:

"Telekinesis. They've built a wall of force around us. On the outside it seems to be rock like the cave wall."

Marah moved, the bosses on his kilt clinking slightly. "When the swine are gone, there's a trap in this hulk leading down to the pipe where your ship is. Now tell us your plan."

Campbell made a short, bitter laugh. "Plan, hell. It's a gamble on a fixed wheel, and you're fools if you play it."

"And if we don't?"

"I'm going anyway. The Kraylens—well, I owe them something."

"Tell us the plan."

He did, in rapid nervous sentences, crouched behind the shielding wall of thought from those alien brains. Marah laughed softly.

"By the gods, little man, you should have been a Keshi!"

"I can think of a lot of things I should have been," said Campbell dourly. "Hey, there goes our wall."

It hadn't been more than four minutes. Long enough for them to look and go away again. There might still be time, before the Spaceguard came.

There was, just. The getaway couldn't have been more perfectly timed. Campbell grinned, feeding power into his jets with exquisite skill.

CITADEL OF LOST SHIPS

He didn't have a Chinaman's chance. He thought probably the gypsies had less than that of coming through. But the Kraylens weren't going to rot in the slave-pens of Lhi because of Roy Campbell.

Not while Roy Campbell was alive to think about it. And that, of course, might not be long.

He sent the Fitts-Sothern shooting toward the night side of Venus, in full view and still throttled down. The Spaceguard ships, nine fast patrol boats, took out after him, giving Romany the go-by. No use stopping there. No mistaking that lean, black ship, or whose hands were on the controls.

Campbell stroked the firing keys, and the Fitts-Sothern purred under him like a cat. Just for a second he couldn't see clearly.

"I'm sorry, old girl," he said. "But that's how it has to be."

*

It was a beautiful chase. The Guard ships pulled every trick they knew, and they knew plenty. Campbell hunched over the keys, sweating, his dark face set in a grin that held no mirth. Only his hands moved, with nervous, delicate speed.

It was the ship that did it. They slapped tractors on her, and she broke them. They tried to encircle her, and she walked away from them. That slight edge of power, that narrow margin of speed, pulled Roy Campbell away from what looked like instant, easy capture.

He got into the shadow, and then the Spaceguard began to get scared as well as angry. They stopped trying to capture him. They unlimbered their blasters and went to work.

Campbell was breathing hard now, through his teeth. His dark skin was oiled with sweat, pulled tight over the bones and the ridges of muscle and the knotted veins. Deliberately, he slowed a little.

34

A bolt flamed past the starboard ports. He slowed still more, and veered the slightest bit. The Fitts-Sothern was alive under his hands.

He didn't speak when the next bolt struck her. Not even to curse. He didn't know he was crying until he tasted the salt on his lips. He got up out of the pilot's seat, and then he said one word:

"*Judas!*"

The follow-up of the first shot blasted the control panel. It knocked him back across the cockpit, seared and scorched from the fusing metal. He got up, somehow, and down the passage to the lock compartment. There was a lot of blood running from his cheek, but he didn't care.

He could feel the ship dying under him. The timers were shot. She was running away in a crazy, blind spiral, racking her plates apart.

He climbed into his vac-suit. It was a special one, black even to the helmet, with a super-powerful harness-rocket with a jet illegally baffled. He hoped his hands weren't too badly burned.

The ship checked brutally, flinging him hard into the bulkhead. Tractors! He clawed toward the lock, an animal whimper in his throat. He hoped he wasn't going to be sick inside the helmet.

The panel opened. Air blasted him out, into jet-black space. The tiny spearing flame of the harness-rocket flickered briefly and died, unnoticed among the trailing fires of the derelict.

Campbell lay quite still in the blackened suit. The Spaceguard ships flared by, playing the Fitts-Sothern like a tarpon on the lines of their tractor beams. Campbell closed his eyes and cursed them, slowly and without expression, until the tightness in his throat choked him off.

He let them get a long way off. Then he pressed the plunger of the rocket, heading down for the night-shrouded swamps of Tehara Province.

He retained no very clear memory of the trip. Once, when he was quite low, a spaceship blazed by over him, heading toward Lhi. There were still about eight hours' darkness over the swamps.

He landed, eventually, in a clearing he was pretty sure only he knew about. He'd used it before when he'd had stuff to fence in Lhi and wasn't sure who owned the town at the time. He'd learned to be careful about those things.

There was a ship there now, a smallish trader of the inter-lunar type. He stared at it, not really believing it was there. Then, just in time, he got the helmet off.

When the world stopped turning over, he was lying with his head in Stella Moore's lap. She had changed her tunic for plain spaceman's black, and it made her face look whiter and lovelier in its frame of black hair. Her lips were still sullen, and still red.

Campbell sat up and kissed them. He felt much better. Not good, but he thought he'd live. Stella laughed and said, "Well! You're recovering."

He said, "Sister, you're good medicine for anything." A hand which he recognized as Marah's materialized out of the indigo gloom. It had a flask in it. Campbell accepted it gladly. Presently the icy deadness around his stomach thawed out and he could see things better.

He got up, rather unsteadily, and fumbled for a cigarette. His shirt had been mostly blown and charred off of him and his hands hurt like hell. Stella gave him a smoke and a light. He sucked it in gratefully and said:

"Okay, kids. Are we all ready?"

They were.

*

Campbell led off. He drained the flask and was pleased to find himself firing on all jets again. He felt empty and relaxed and ready for anything. He hoped the liquor wouldn't wear off too soon.

There was a path threaded through the hammocks, the bogs and potholes and reeds and *liha*-trees. Only Campbell, who had made it, could have followed it. Remembering his blind stumbling in the mazes of Romany, he felt pleased about that. He said, rather smugly:

"Be careful not to slip. How'd you fix the getaway?"

Marah made a grim little laugh. "Romany was a madhouse, hunting for you. Some of the hot-headed boys started minor wars over policy on top of that. Tredrick had to use most of his men to keep order. Besides, of course, he thought we were beaten on the Kraylen question."

"There were only four men guarding the locks," said Stella. "Marah and a couple of the Paniki boys took care of them."

Campbell remembered the spaceship flashing toward Lhi. He told them about it. "Could be Tredrick, coming to supervise our defeat in person." Defeat! It was because he was a little tight, of course, but he didn't think anyone could defeat him this night. He laughed.

Something rippled out of the indigo night to answer his laughter. Something so infinitely sweet and soft that it made him want to cry, and then shocked him with the deep and iron power in it. Campbell looked back over his shoulder. He thought:

"Me, hell. These are the guys who'll do it, if it's done."

Stella was behind him. Beyond her was a thin, small man with four arms. He wore no clothing but his own white fur and his head was crowned with feathery antennae. Even in the blue night the antennae and the man's eyes burned living scarlet.

He came from Callisto and he carried in his four hands a thing vaguely like a harp, only the strings were double banked. It was the harp that had spoken. Campbell hoped it would never speak against him.

Marah brought up the rear, swinging along with no regard for the burden he bore. Over his naked shoulder, Campbell could see the still white face of the Baraki from Titan, the Little Father who had saved them from the hunters. There were tentacles around Marah's big body like white ropes.

Four gypsies and a Public Enemy. Five little people against the Terro-Venusian Coalition. It didn't make sense.

A hot, slow wind stirred the *liha*-trees. Campbell breathed it in, and grinned. "What does?" he wondered, and stooped to part a tangle of branches. There was a stone-lined tunnel beyond.

"Here we go, children. Join hands and make like little mousies." He took Stella's hand in his left. Because it was Stella's he didn't mind the way it hurt. In his right, he held his gun.

V

He led them, quickly and quietly, along the disused branch of an old drainage system that he had used so often as a private entrance. Presently they dropped to a lower level and the conduit system proper.

When the rains were on, the drains would be running full. Now they were only pumping seepage. They waded in pitch darkness, by-passed a pumping station through a side tunnel once used for cold storage by one of Lhi's cautious business men, and then found steep, slippery steps going up.

"Careful," whispered Campbell. He stopped them on a narrow ledge and stood listening. The Callistan murmured, with faint amusement:

"There is no one beyond."

Antennae over ears. Campbell grinned and found a hidden spring. "Lhi is full of these things," he said. "The boys used to keep their little wars going just for fun, and every smart guy had several bolt holes. Maps used to sell high."

They emerged in a very deep, very dark cellar. It was utterly still. Campbell felt a little sad. He could remember when Martian Mak's was the busiest thieves' market in Lhi, and a man could hear the fighting even here. He smiled bitterly and led the way upstairs.

Presently they looked down on the main gate, the main square, and the slave pens of Lhi. The surrounding streets were empty, the buildings mostly dark. The Coalition had certainly cleaned up when it took over the town. It was horribly depressing.

Campbell pointed. "Reception committee. Tredrick radioed, anyway. One'll get you twenty he followed it up in person."

The gate was floodlighted over a wide area and there were a lot of tough-looking men with heavy-duty needle guns. In this day of anaesthetic charges you could do a lot of effective shooting without doing permanent damage. There were more lights and more men by the slave pens.

Campbell couldn't see much over the high stone walls of the pens. Vague movement, the occasional flash of a brilliant crest. He had known the Kraylens would be there. It was the only place in Lhi where you could imprison a lot of people and be sure of keeping them.

Campbell's dark face was cruel. "Okay," he said. "Let's go."

*

Down the stone steps to the entrance. Stella's quick breathing in the hot darkness, the rhythmic clink of the bosses on Marah's kilt. Campbell saw the eyes of the Callistan harper, glowing red and angry. He realized he was sweating. He had forgotten his burns.

CITADEL OF LOST SHIPS

Stella opened the heavy steel-sheathed door. Quietly, slowly. The Baraki whispered, "Put me down."

Marah set him gently on the stone floor. He folded in upon himself, tentacles around white, rubbery flesh. His single eye burned with a cold phosphorescence.

He whispered, "Now."

The Callistan harper went to the door. Reflected light painted him briefly, white fur and scarlet crest and outlandish harp, and the glowing, angry eyes.

He vanished. Out of nowhere the harp began to sing.

Through the partly opened door Campbell had a clear view of the square and the gate. In all that glare of light on empty stone nothing moved. And yet the music rippled out.

The guards. Campbell could see the startled glitter of their eyeballs in the light. There was nothing to shoot at. The harping was part of the night, as all-enveloping and intangible.

Campbell shivered. A pulse beat like a trip-hammer under his jaw. Stella's voice came to him, a faint breath out of the darkness.

"The Baraki is shielding him with thought. A wall of force that turns the light."

The edge of the faint light touched her cheek, the blackness of her hair. Marah crouched beyond her, motionless. His hook glinted dully, curved and cruel.

They were getting only the feeble backwash of the harping. The Callistan was aiming his music outward. Campbell felt it sweep and tremble, blend with the hot slow wind and the indigo sky.

It was some trick of vibrations, some diabolical thrusting of notes against the brain like fingers, to press and control. Something about the double-banked strings thrumming against each other under the cunning of four skilled hands. But it was like witchcraft.

40

"The Harp of Dagda," whispered Stella Moore, and the Irish music in her voice was older than time. The Scot in Campbell answered it.

Somewhere outside a man cursed, thickly, like one drugged with sleep and afraid of it. A gun went off with a sharp slapping sound. Some of the guards had fallen down.

The harp sang louder, throbbing along the grey stones. It was the slow wind, the heat, the deep blue night. It was sleep.

The floodlights blazed on empty stone, and the guards slept.

The Baraki sighed and shivered and closed his eye. Campbell saw the Callistan harper standing in the middle of the square, his scarlet crest erect, striking the last thrumming note.

Campbell straightened, catching his breath in a ragged sob. Marah picked up the Baraki. He was limp, like a tired child. Stella's eyes were glistening and strange. Campbell went out ahead of them.

It was a long way across the square, in the silence and the glaring lights. Campbell thought the harp was a nice weapon. It didn't attract attention because everyone who heard it slept.

He flung back the three heavy bars of the slave gate. The pain of his burned hands jarred him out of the queer mood the harping and his Celtic blood had put on him. He began to think again.

"Hurry!" he snarled at the Kraylens. "Hurry up!" They came pouring out of the gate. Men, women with babies, little children. Their crests burned in the sullen glare.

Campbell pointed to Marah. "Follow him." They recognized him, tried to speak, but he cursed them on. And then an old man said,

"My son."

Campbell looked at him, and then down at the stones. "For God's sake, Father, hurry." A hand touched his shoulder gently. He looked up again, and grinned. He couldn't see anything. "Get the hell on, will you?" Somebody found the switch and the nearer lights went out.

41

CITADEL OF LOST SHIPS

The hand pressed his shoulder, and was gone. He shook his head savagely. The Kraylens were running now, toward the house. And then, suddenly, Marah yelled.

Men were running into the square. Eight or ten of them, probably the bodyguard of the burly grey-haired man who led them. Beside the grey-haired man was Tredrick, Overchief of the Terran Quarter of Romany.

*

They were startled. They hadn't been expecting this. Campbell's battle-trained eye saw that. Probably they had been making a routine tour of inspection and just stumbled onto the crash-out.

Campbell fired, from the hip. Anaesthetic needles sprayed into the close-packed group. Two of them went down. The rest scattered, dropping flat. Campbell wished there had been time to kill the gate lights. At least, the shadows made shooting tricky.

He bent over and began to run, guarding the rear of the Kraylen's line. Stella, in the cover of the doorway, was laying down a methodical wall of needles. Campbell grinned.

Some of the Kraylens caught it and had to be carried. That slowed things down. Campbell's gun clicked empty. He shoved in another clip, cursing his burned fingers. A charge sang by him, close enough to stir his hair. He fired again, blanketing the whole sector where the men lay. He wished he could blow Tredrick's head off.

The Kraylens were vanishing into the house. Marah and the Callistan had gone ahead, leading them. Campbell groaned. Speed was what they needed. Speed. A child, separated from his mother in the rush, knelt on the stones and shrieked. Campbell picked him up and ran on.

Enemy fire was slackening. Stella was doing all right. The last of the Kraylens shoved through the door. Campbell bounded up the steps. Stella got up off her belly and smiled at him. Her eyes shone. They were halfway through the door when the cold voice said behind them,

"There are lethal needles in my gun. You had better stop."

Campbell turned slowly. His face was wooden. Tredrick stood at the bottom of the steps. He must have crawled around the edge of the square, where the shadows were thick under the walls.

"Drop your gun, Campbell. And you, Stella Moore."

Campbell dropped it. Tredrick might be bluffing about those needles. But a Mickey at this stage of the game would be just as fatal. Stella's gun clattered beside him. She didn't say anything, but her face was coldly murderous.

Tredrick said evenly, "You might as well call them back, Campbell. You led them in, but you're not going to lead them out."

It was funny, Campbell thought, how a man's voice could be so cold when his eyes had fire in them. He said sullenly,

"Okay, Tredrick. You win. But what's the big idea behind this?"

Tredrick's face might have been cut from granite, except for the feral eyes. "I was born on Romany. I froze and starved in those rotten hulks. I hated it. I hated the darkness, the loneliness, the uncertainty. But when I said I hated it, I got a beating.

"Everybody else thought it was worth it. I didn't. They talked about freedom, but Romany was a prison to me. I wanted to grow, and I was stifled inside it. Then I got an idea.

"If I could rule Romany and make a treaty with the Coalition, I'd have money and power. And I could fix it so no more kids would be brought up that way, cold and hungry and scared.

43

"Marah opposed me, and then the Kraylens became an issue." Tredrick smiled, but there was no mirth or softness in it. "It's a good thing. The Coalition can take of Marah and you others who were mixed up in this. My way is clear."

Stella Moore said softly between her teeth, "They'll never forgive you for turning Romany people over to the *latniks*. There'll be war."

Tredrick nodded soberly. "No great change is made without bloodshed. I'm sorry for that. But Romany will be happier."

"We don't ask to be happy. We only ask to be free."

Campbell said wearily, "Stella, take the kid, will you?" He held out the little Kraylen, droopy and quiet now. She looked at him in quick alarm. His feet were spread but not steady, his head sunk forward.

She took the child. Campbell's knees sagged. One seared arm in a tattered green sleeve came up to cover his face. The other groped blindly along the wall. He dropped, rather slowly, to his knees.

The groping hand fell across the gun by Stella's foot. In one quick sweep of motion Campbell got it, threw it, and followed it with his own body.

*

The gun missed, but it came close enough to Tredrick's face to make him move his head. The involuntary muscular contraction of his whole body spoiled his aim. The charge went past Campbell into the wall.

They crashed down together on the stones. Campbell gripped Tredrick's wrist, knew he couldn't hold it, let go with one hand and slashed backward with his elbow at Tredrick's face.

The gun let off again, harmlessly, Tredrick groaned. His arm was weaker. Campbell thrashed over and got his knee on it. Tredrick's other fist was savaging his already tortured body.

Campbell brought his fist down into Tredrick's face. He did it twice, and wept and cursed because he was suddenly too weak to lift his arm again. Tredrick was bleeding, but far from out. His gun was coming up again. He didn't have much play, but enough.

Campbell set his teeth. He couldn't even see Tredrick, but he swung again. He never knew whether he connected or not.

Something thrummed past his head. He couldn't say he heard it. It was more like feeling. But it was something deadly, and strange. Tredrick didn't make a sound. Campbell knew suddenly that he was dead.

He got up, very slow, shaking and cold. The Callistan harper stood in the doorway. He was lowering his hands, and his eyes were living coals. He didn't say anything. Neither did Stella. But she laughed, and the child stirred and whimpered in her arms.

Campbell went to her. She looked at him with queer eyes and whispered, "I called him with my mind. I knew he'd kill."

He took her face in his two hands. "Listen, Stella. You've got to lead them back. You've got to touch my mind with yours and let me guide you that way, back to the ship."

Her eyes widened sharply. "But you can come. He's dead. You're free now."

"No." He could feel her throat quiver under his hands. Her blood was beating. So was his. He said harshly,

"You fool, do you think they'll let you get away with this? You're tackling the Coalition. They can't afford to look silly. They've got to have a scapegoat, something to save face!

45

"Romany, so far, is beyond planetary control. Slap your tractors on her, tow her out. Clear out to Saturn if you have to. Nobody saw the Callistan. Nobody saw anybody but me and the Kraylens and an unidentifiable somebody up here on the porch. Nobody, that is, but Tredrick, and he won't talk. Do you understand?"

She did, but she was still rebellious. Her sullen lips were angry, her eyes bright with tears and challenging. "But you, Roy!"

He took his hands away. "Damn you, woman! If I hide out on Romany I bring you into Spaceguard jurisdiction. I'll be trapped, and Romany's last chance to stay free will be gone."

She said stubbornly, "But you can get away. There are ships."

"Oh, sure. But the Kraylens are there. You can't hide them. The Coalition will search Romany. They'll ask questions. I tell you they've got to have a goat!"

He was really weak, now. He hoped he could hold out. He hoped he wouldn't do anything disgraceful. He turned away from her, looking out at the square. Some of the guards were beginning to stir.

"Will you go?" he said. "Will you get to hell out?"

She put her hand on him. "Roy...."

He jerked away. His dark face was set and cruel. "Do you have to make it harder? Do you think I want to rot on Phobos in their stinking mines, with shackles on my feet?" He swung around, challenging her with savage eyes.

"How else do you think Romany is going to stay free? You can't go on playing cat and mouse with the big shots this way. They're getting sick of it. They'll pass laws and tie you down. Somebody's got to spread Romany all over the Solar System. Somebody's got to pull a publicity campaign that'll make the great dumb public sit up and think. If public opinion's with you, you're safe."

He smiled. "I'm big news, sister. I'm Roy Campbell. I can splash your lousy little mess of tin cans all over with glamour, so the great dumb public won't let a hair of your little head be hurt. If you want to, you can raise a statue to me in the Council hall.

"And now will you for God's sake go?"

*

She wasn't crying. Her gray eyes had lights in them. "You're wonderful, Roy. I didn't realize how wonderful."

He was ashamed, then. "Nuts. In my racket you don't expect to get away with it forever. Besides, I'm an old dog. I know my way around. I have a little dough saved up. I won't be in for long."

"I hope not," she said. "Oh, Roy, it's so stupid! Why do Earthmen have to change everything they lay their hands on?"

He looked at Tredrick, lying on the stones. His voice came slow and sombre.

"They're building, Stella. When they're finished they'll have a big, strong, prosperous world extending all across the planets, and the people who belong to that world will be happy.

"But before you can build you have to grade and level, destroy the things that get in your way. We're the things—the tree—stumps and the rocks that grew one way and can't be changed.

"They're building, Stella. They're growing. You can't stop that. In the end, it'll be a good thing, I suppose. But right now, for us...."

He broke off. He thrust her roughly inside and locked the steel-sheathed door. "You've got to go now."

It was dark, and hot. The Kraylen child whimpered. He could feel Stella close to him. He found her lips and kissed them.

He said, "So long, kid. And about that statue. You'd better wait till I come back to pose for it."

His voice became a longing whisper. "*And I'll be back!*" he promised.

Lightning Source UK Ltd.
Milton Keynes UK
UKHW011904300921
391472UK00001B/104